NEW BOOKS FOR NEW READERS

Phyllis MacAdam, *General Editor*

Heartwood

Nikky Finney

THE UNIVERSITY PRESS OF KENTUCKY

Publication of this volume was made possible in part by a grant
from the National Endowment for the Humanities.

Scholarly publisher for the Commonwealth,
serving Bellarmine College, Berea College, Centre
College of Kentucky, Eastern Kentucky University,
The Filson Club Historical Society, Georgetown College,
Kentucky Historical Society, Kentucky State University,
Morehead State University, Transylvania University,
University of Kentucky, University of Louisville,
and Western Kentucky University.

Editorial and Sales Offices: The University Press of Kentucky
663 South Limestone Street, Lexington, Kentucky 40508-4008

01 00 99 98 97   5 4 3 2 1

Library of Congress Cataloging-in-Publication Data

Finney, Nikky.
    Heartwood / Nikky Finney.
        p.   cm. — (New books for new readers)
    ISBN 0-8131-0910-8 (paper : alk. paper)
    1. Afro-Americans—Kentucky—Fiction. 2. Readers for
new literates I. Title. II. Series.
    PS3556.I53H43   1997
    813'.54—dc21   97-25201

Manufactured in the United States of America

Contents

Foreword

The Kentucky Humanities Council began its New Books for New Readers project because Kentucky's adult literacy students want books that recognize their intelligence and experience while meeting their need for simplicity in writing. The first nine titles in the New Books for New Readers series have helped many adult students open a window on the wonderful world of literacy. At the same time, the New Books, with their plain language and compelling stories of Kentucky history and culture, have found a wider audience among accomplished readers of all ages who recognize a good read when they see one. As we publish the tenth New Book, we thank our authors and our readers, who together have proved that New Books and the humanities are for everyone.

This volume was made possible, in part, by the continuing assistance of the Scripps Howard Foundation through the *Kentucky Post* and through support from the *Louisville Courier-Journal,* the Moninger Schmidt Fund, and friends of the Kentucky Humanities Council. The cosponsorship of the Kentucky Department for Libraries and Archives and the Kentucky Literacy Commission has been essential to our undertaking. We are also grateful for the advice and support provided to us by the University Press of Kentucky. All of these agencies share our commitment to the important role reading books plays in the lives of the people of our Commonwealth.

Virginia G. Smith, Executive Director
Kentucky Humanities Council

Preface

When you peel back the bark of a tree, the hardest wood, tucked deep inside, is called the heartwood. This wood is the heart of the tree itself, both its soul and its center. This story called *Heartwood* has some of the most plain-talking, stubborn, and outspoken people I've ever met. My hope is that they will remind you of someone you know or something you have witnessed in your own life. These people and their stories are the heartwood of their communities. They put a human face to the land they live on and the air they breathe.

This story takes place in Kentucky, the state that I have called home for the past six years. The ideas and sounds come from what I have seen and heard while I have lived here. The hope as well as the hurt found in these pages is important to the fabric of this book. My desire as storyteller is simple: that what these characters talk about and what they do to each other might move you to take on something controversial in your own life or choose not to remain silent about something that needs your goodness and input. Fiction should reflect life in all its majesty and madness.

I have never felt more honored to write a piece of work than *Heartwood*. I have never been more affected and changed as a human being than I was when I sat with my circle of critics and editors: Bessie Chestnut, Margaret Lane, Rosa Stonestreet, Alice Waite, and Alona Johnson, members of Lexington's Operation Read, brilliant human beings new to the written word, and Sandra Parrish and Charlotte Pyles of Lexington/Fayette County Mayor's Training Center Adult Education program. These are editors who cared enough to laugh, get angry, and share with me every human emotion about what I have to say. This is what writing and reading must, and should, be all about. I hope that what you find on these pages makes you talk and feel and act with your heart in mind.

Thank you Phyllis MacAdam, Anne Keenan, and Bertie J. Harris for your invaluable guidance. Thank you Humanities Council for continuing to care that the truth and magic of books be available to us all.

The Secret of Luketown

Trina Sims waited at the train station. She leaned back easy on the hood of her car. She crossed her legs at the ankles and folded her long brown arms softly at the waist. She felt good standing out in the sun, even if she wasn't sure how long she would have to wait. It had stormed hard the night before. The morning air was clear and clean. She took in a long deep breath and pushed her new sunglasses up tight to her face.

There were other women waiting in the parking lot, but there were no other black women. Some of the people were waiting by themselves, just like Trina, but none of them had on sunglasses. Trina's glasses were round and shiny with somebody's long fancy name written out on the side of them.

She didn't know or care whose name it was as long as it was there. The name on the side meant they were not just regular sunglasses. That was important to Trina, who didn't see herself as just regular either.

Trina was a brown-skinned woman with short pressed hair. All around her eyes this morning she looked like a movie star or at least somebody who had a good secret to tell. She smiled when she thought about herself as somebody with a secret. Thinking this gave her private space away from everybody else in the world. She liked having a little room so she could make good decisions and think for herself. She liked wearing her sunglasses, and she didn't care what anybody else thought.

The 9:25 train was late this morning, and lots of people were waiting behind the wire fence for any sight of it. Sometimes she could feel them looking at her. Sometimes she thought she could feel them trying to figure out who she was and where she was from. Nobody had ever seen a black woman with such fancy sunglasses around Bluebell, Kentucky. Trina just kept her eyes in front of her and decided to let them go on and wonder who she was. She wasn't trying to move into the neighborhood. She was only visiting. Trina just kept staring at the spot where she hoped the train might soon come to a stop.

Bluebell, Kentucky, was the only train station for a hundred miles, so strangers passed through all the time. Some folks sat inside their cars and waited. Other folks were outside, leaning back, feeling good in the sun, just like Trina. Nobody spoke to her while she stood there. But she could hear them talking to each other about how a hot April meant a hot summer. It was good and warm, just like Trina liked it. It was perfect weather for sunglasses.

Standing out in the sun and waiting on a train that was bringing a stranger made Trina think about how everything was about to change in her life. How she was quitting her job at Moore Farm and going into business for herself. It was an old dream that she hoped was about to come true. The classes she had been taking at the county training school had given her the courage to finally do it. She didn't know what the future would be. She only knew she didn't want to spend the rest of her life doing what she had been doing for 10 long years. Here she was 29 years old and still helping grown people take care of their own lives. She didn't want to reach 30 thinking the only thing she was good at was helping rich people count their money every day. The more she thought about it, the more she smiled to herself. Her own life could use a little help, and maybe she could start with her cigarette smoking habit.

She lifted a cigarette out of the pack that had been resting on the hood of the car. She lit it with the silver lighter that her fingers had been playing with inside her dress pocket. Her lips let the smoke go up, and the wind quickly took it behind her somewhere. Just as she looked down at her wrist to see what time it was, she finally heard the train coming.

Some of the children who had been playing in the parking lot ran toward the fence to see. They moved against the wire wall like a flock of small birds. They pushed their tiny feet and fingers through the holes and held on, hoping to see what they had only been able to hear so far. The train pulled to a stop right in front of them. They let go of the fence all at once and ran to the opening in the gate. Trina watched the gate wave a little from their weight and tremble finally to a stop.

One by one, the travelers climbed down out of the train door. In their arms they had bags and sacks of different things. A small crowd of waving people moved toward the gate to greet them, but Trina never left the hood of her car. From her pocket she pulled a picture of the woman she had been sent to pick up, looked at it quickly, then put it back. Behind her dark sunglasses, her soft brown eyes bounced from one face to the next looking for the right one. Then a young white woman with thick red hair pulled back in a ponytail got off the train. Trina squinted her eyes and fixed her glasses back up tight on her nose. The woman walked down the steps and came closer. Trina could see she was holding a piece of yellow paper tight in her hand. She was carrying a suitcase and wearing a yellow sweater that was too warm for the hot day. The woman was the last one off the train.

Before the red-haired woman walked all the way through the gate, she slowed down and turned around a few times. She stopped and looked at the few cars that were left outside the gate. Then she walked toward Trina. Trina dropped her cigarette on the ground, blew out the last of the smoke, and bit her lip. Without looking she moved her foot around on the ground, hoping to step on the butt and put it out. She didn't turn around yet, even when she heard the young woman moving around right behind her.

"Hey! Hey you! Hey! I'm here for the job at Moore Farm. Did Miss Dorothy Moore send you to pick me up?"

Trina, in her fancy sunglasses, slowly got up and turned around. "Are you Jennifer Bryan?"

The woman acted like she wasn't sure how she felt about Trina saying her name. "Yeah . . . Jenny, Jenny Bryan, yeah, that's me. But they told me to expect a man named Fuller. Dorothy Moore said somebody named Fuller was coming to get me. She said to be sure and ask for him."

Trina put her hands up in the air. "Easy, Lady. Just calm yourself down. I don't usually do the pick-ups. Fuller was coming, but one of the new horses got out this morning. He got changed to fixing fences, and I got the call to come get you."

"You work for Miss Moore?" the woman questioned Trina.

"I do. But not for long." Trina moved to the back of the car and opened the trunk. "My name's Trina, Trina Sims. I'm the one leaving the farm. It's my job Miss Moore wants to hire you for. How you do?" Trina held out a hand to shake.

But Jenny Bryan held on tight to her bag with both hands. She looked away from the black woman standing in front of her holding out her hand. Then she looked around at the almost empty train yard. Trina dropped her hand quickly and turned away. She moved some old clothes from one side of the trunk to the other side. Her voice had completely changed the next time she spoke.

"Miss Moore said that the place where you come from, Stone Creek, only has white people living there. Is that true?"

The woman with red hair looked at Trina. "Yeah, that's true. But that don't mean nothing." She laughed nervously.

"Daddy used to say 'everything means something.'" Trina waited before she went on. "In fact, Miss Moore said your town *won't let* black folks live there. Is that true?"

"Yes, that's true. But . . ."

"She said you might be nervous about me coming to pick you up. You're not nervous are you?"

Jenny didn't answer her right away. She laughed out of the corner of her mouth. "Nervous! I ain't nervous. It's just been a long trip, and I didn't know it was you coming, that's all."

"Look, Jennifer, Jenny Bryan, or whatever your name is, before we get in this car and move an inch, let's you and me get this out right now. I don't bite my tongue. I say what's on my mind." Trina stood up real straight. "Just because you ain't never been around black folks does not mean you got to learn how to think and talk all over again. We didn't fall out the sky like something from another planet. God put us all here at the same time in the same way. Black folks drive cars and eat grits just like other folks, and sometimes we even wear big fancy sunglasses, if we want to." Trina pushed her glasses back tight on her face.

The woman with the ponytail looked away, then back at Trina. Trina mumbled something to herself and left the trunk open. She went back around to the driver's side of the car and got in. She turned the key to wake up the engine. The old Buick started up easy with a tiny puff of gray smoke. Trina pushed the pedal down a few times until the engine sound was smooth and strong. She lit another cigarette and watched in the mirror as Jenny Bryan threw her things in the trunk, closed it, and got in slowly beside her.

The 1976 baby blue Wildcat pulled out of the parking lot and started out on the highway toward Taylorsville. The car had been a gift from Trina's brother, Melvin, who was always taking something old and rusty and making it pretty again. He was the one who gave her the sunglasses too. He said the glasses and the car went together like a hand and a glove. He was the one who had told her that the glasses made her look like she was somebody from somewhere else, which meant she had lots of secrets to tell.

Jenny kept looking over at Trina. She probably wanted to ask her whose fancy car this was because she knew it couldn't be hers, Trina thought.

"Uh, Trina," Jenny Bryan said. "I know I was asking you a lot of questions back there. I didn't mean nothing by it. You gotta be careful these days, that's all. It didn't help any that you got those big old sunglasses on. I can hardly see your face. I didn't know who you were. You could have been a murderer or crazy or anything."

Trina's voice didn't wait her turn. "You come in here wearing that big yellow sweater hot as it is, and I don't ask you why. But maybe that should make me scared of you. Maybe you're hiding something up your sleeves from me." Jenny touched the sleeves of her sweater and pulled them down a little more.

Trina kept on talking. "A big yellow sweater on as hot a day as this. And anyway you *still* don't know who I might be. Anybody could be a murderer or crazy. That's not the point. The point is *you* come riding in here from a place where being me is against the law. And even though I knew your name, it still wasn't enough. The real point is you coming from a place where nobody like me can lay a head down at night across town from somebody like you and just plain go to sleep like everybody else. But somebody like me has to stop what I'm doing just to be sent to pick you up from the train station. Just because you decide to leave your fantasy world and come out here looking for a job in the real world."

Jenny had turned away and was trying her best to leave the car by way of her eyes. But Trina's hard words kept bringing her back inside of herself. "Come on, now. Let's be real about it. The reason you didn't want to get in my car was because I'm black. It didn't have anything to do with my sunglasses. I wasn't born this morning." Trina held the wheel tightly with both hands as they went around a curve too fast. The tires made a loud screeching sound, and she slowed down and apologized.

"I'm sorry. I don't usually drive so bad. Now I bet you really think I'm trying to kill you don't you?"

"No, Trina, listen, I'm sorry. You're right about what happened back there." Jenny Bryan smiled and talked nervously. "I didn't make the rules in Stone Creek, Trina. They were there when I got there twenty-five years ago. I guess I was just kinda born right in the middle of them. I never really thought about them too much. Never had to."

"There's an old rule that says, 'Do unto others as you would have them do unto you.' That's a good rule, Jenny Bryan. Those things y'all got in Stone Creek are some kind of man-made law, something made by one man to keep another man in his place. A golden rule is way bigger and more important than any law. At least that's what my mama taught me. She said a rule comes from God, and a law is what is man-made, and there's plenty of corrupt men walking around. So you might not have made the laws in Stone Creek, Jenny Bryan, but it seems to me you agree with them because you stay there and live by them. Don't y'all know what year it is? Ain't y'all heard of Martin Luther King Jr., or at least Oprah Winfrey? Everybody, everywhere, at least has heard of Oprah."

Jenny hesitated before she answered, and Trina started laughing out loud.

"What are you laughing at?"

"I'm laughing at you, girl. Come on now. You know good and well that everyday at three o'clock every white man, woman, and child with a television set in Stone Creek runs home and pulls the curtains and locks their door and watches Oprah in secret."

Jenny let out a little laugh but not as big as Trina's. Trina beat the steering wheel around the whole curve of the mountain. Slowly she got herself back together.

Trina shook her head and pushed her glasses back up on her face. Suddenly she looked hurt and a little lost. "You know what, Jenny Bryan? There are some things I hope I never understand, like how there happens to be, in this day and age, a big old town full of people who hate me just because God gave me the brown skin out his closet and gave them the white one. That's the saddest thing I ever heard of in my whole life."

Jenny's eyes went back outside through the window. And at that same moment Trina began to whistle, low at first, but then sometimes she would blow strong and pretty just like her Uncle Jack had taught her to do when she was a little girl. She always whistled when she needed to work something out in her head. A few more miles down the road and they both leaned back into the seat and relaxed a little. Trina seemed to forget about her sadness. She was tapping her finger against the steering wheel.

"It takes too much energy to stay mad. You ever notice that, Jenny Bryan?"

"Never really noticed that, not really, but I think you're right."

When Trina's eyes saw the sign with one arrow pointing to "Taylorsville 50 miles" and the other pointing the opposite direction to "Luketown 10 miles," she suddenly got an idea.

At the first railroad crossing Trina made a quick right off the paved road onto a dirt one. The speed of the turn made Jenny jump. She had noticed the sign and how Taylorsville was pointing in the other direction. Her voice was too loud again.

"This ain't the way, Trina." Jenny looked afraid. "Where— where are we going?"

Trina smiled and patted the steering wheel. "Melvin, that's my brother, he said when I wear these glasses I look like I might be from some kind of secret place. I love when he says that about me. Imagine that, me, little old plain me, from a secret place." Trina smiled again. "Do you think he might be right, Jenny Bryan?"

"I . . . I don't know. Maybe."

"I know he's right. I know it." Trina took in a deep breath. "We are going to the place where I was born, Luketown, U.S.A. I need to pick something up from Mama on the way back to Taylorsville. You don't mind do you? You ever heard of Luketown, Jenny Bryan?"

"Never did."

Trina smiled again. "Well, I think it's time you see Luketown. Something tells me it's a lot like Stone Creek."

The two women looked at each other and then turned away. Trina was smiling and Jenny was not.

The old Buick took the last curve. Jenny saw "Luketown Population 196" painted on a wooden sign that sat on the side of the road. The end of the curve put them on a wide dirt street lined on both sides with tiny shotgun houses all painted ice-cream colors. The yards were full of green plants and chairs. Cars of all shapes and sizes ran from one end of the long street to the other. It was quiet, and people were everywhere.

"Welcome to Luketown, Jenny Bryan. The first and only all-black town in the great tobacco state of Kentucky. Sweet home to black folks for over one hundred dark and lovely years."

Jenny Bryan wasn't smiling. In fact she was holding onto the car seat with both hands. Her fingernails were cutting into the plastic. She was looking all around her now. Her eyes seemed scared of whatever was moving around in her head, more than what was coming and going on the quiet, tree-lined main street of Luketown, Kentucky.

Trina drove up the old dirt street about two blocks before pulling the car over to the side. She stopped right next to a tiny wooden shop. The sign outside read "Queen Ida's Hair-Doing House of Waves." A dog was barking and running a cat across somebody's yard. "I won't be long, Jenny Bryan. We'll be back on our way before you can say Stone Creek five times."

Trina cut the engine and made her quick steps up to the front door. She waved and spoke to people she knew. Before she went inside she looked back one more time to check on Jenny Bryan. She knew it was the first time the red-headed woman from Stone Creek had ever been to an all-black town. Trina thought she might be a little scared at first, but she knew that sitting there would be just the chair Jenny needed to see the secrets of Trina's most favorite place in the world.

Sitting in the car alone, Jenny felt her heart pounding loud like a drum. As she waited, she looked around to try and see what kind of a place this was, this place that a woman she had never seen before had brought her to.

Up and down the long street black people were everywhere doing something. She had never seen so many black people before. She had never been away from Stone Creek before this morning. She had grown up hearing stories from her grandpa and her own daddy about how proud they were of their all-white town. They told Jenny that back in 1907, white men had killed or run every black man, woman, and child out of Stone Creek. Her daddy told her that they planned to keep it that way. Jenny sat there now wondering for the first time if that was a true story.

Jenny had never thought about it much until now. She had never felt sorry for black people, but she didn't hate them like her daddy did either. She decided that the truth was that she had never felt anything at all for black people. Trina was the first black woman she had ever met face to face. Up until now, that's just the way things had been in her life, and she had accepted that way without question.

And here it was just the first few hours after leaving home, and Jenny was already thinking about things she had never thought about before in her whole 25 years of life. She pushed her long, yellow sweater sleeves up a little. The big blue bruises that were inside her arms were still there. She took a deep breath and pulled the sleeves back down quickly. She knew how long it usually took before they disappeared. She just hated that they were there this weekend while she was away.

This morning as the train had moved away from Stone Creek, Jenny knew she had to leave it for good. She wanted to get this new job and start a new life. She was scared but not scared enough to give up her idea of leaving Stone Creek. She just had to make sure that Taylorsville was the right place.

There in the car waiting on Trina, Jenny could hear the different voices of her family running through her mind clear as spring water. Her daddy had always told her black people were the worst of all people. She didn't think she believed that, but for some reason all she could hear right then was his voice saying that. Jenny remembered the time when he had told her in a low serious voice that black people weren't even really human like other folks.

She put her finger in her ear and tried to shake him out of her mind. As Jenny remembered some more of what he had said, she didn't feel so safe. She rolled her open window up tight all the way. But at the same time her eyes couldn't help moving down the whole wide street around her. She looked curiously at everything there was to see.

The big oak and maple trees that sat on both sides of the street were just getting their new leaves and starting to bloom. Black people of all ages were sitting out under the trees or leaning over their fences. They were talking and laughing with each other from one porch to another porch, just like people did back in Stone Creek.

One old woman was sweeping her yard the old way, with a hand-tied broom, just like Jenny's grandmother used to do. She hadn't thought about that broom in a long time. And there was an old man with an old cap and a long beard. He was popping open the top of a beer can and maybe cussing about the wars he had fought in. There were other people coming and going, walking and just plain living. Jenny's heart began to relax a little.

From the front seat of Trina's car and for the first time in her life, Jenny didn't see anything so different about black people and white people. She leaned back in her seat and thought about what she was finally learning for herself and for her new life, with her own two eyes. She tried to understand what she was seeing because everything she had ever been told about black people did not fit this picture in front of her. She was still scared, but what she saw began to make her think just a little bit different than the way she woke up thinking that morning.

Slowly Jenny's hand went to the window crank. She turned it down just enough to hear the air moving outside. With the sweet air came more of the sounds of life. There were young women out in front of some of the houses now. They were all shades of black and brown. Some had their hands down in the dirt, pulling up weeds and planting things. Some were leaning and talking to the other ones. Trina was so right. It could have been Stone Creek, Kentucky, except for the skin color. The work that was being done, the talk and laughter you could hear, the movements here and there were all a language Jenny easily understood.

There was a church down on the corner and on the other side of the street a place called the Fish Basket that had a bright red sign out front. The smell of catfish suddenly came through Jenny's window. The hot fish smell made her remember how hungry she was. She thought about how good a plate of hot catfish and cornbread would be.

A rubber kick ball hit the side window, and Jenny covered her head with her arms, holding her breath. Two laughing boys no more than eight or nine had bumped into the car while playing. They had not seen her sitting inside. All Jenny could hear after that was one man's strong clear voice up the street giving them two seconds to get their butts on home! They saw Jenny as they ran by and yelled out together "Sorry, Lady!" before they took off running up the street after the bouncing ball toward the loud voice.

Then finally the door to the little shop opened. Trina stepped out with a cardboard box of tiny jars in one arm and bags of something else in the other. An older woman all dressed up and wearing a freshly starched apron was holding the door open for her and waving at Jenny like an old friend. "The Queen" was sewn in big letters all across the top of her apron. Jenny slowly raised her hand and waved back.

Trina put her packages in the back before climbing in up front. Jenny had somehow moved to the middle of the car seat, trying to see everything all the way up the street. The shoulders of the two women brushed each other, and Jenny moved quickly back over to her side.

"Oops, sorry. Excuse me," she said.

"Well, now, how did you get way over here in the middle? There must have really been something to look at out on Luketown Street while I was gone." Trina smiled as soon as she sat down and started talking fast.

"That was my mama who came out on the porch. I mean, that was my new business partner." Trina laughed. "You know when I was a little girl she made everything we ever needed. Everything. Even the hair grease we used, she made that too. And what she made always seemed to work better on our hair than anything we ever bought in the grocery store. They didn't make things for black people back then. As far back as I can remember she has made jars and jars of it for other ladies too. Everybody has been telling her for years, 'Ida, you ought to go into the hair oil business.' So that's what we are finally going to do. That's why I took that business class, and that's why I'm quitting my job with Miss Moore, and that's how you got here. Because me and Mama are going into the hair oil business."

Jenny's eyes got wide and excited. "You—you're going into business with your Mama? You're not gonna have a boss or a time clock no more?" Jenny sighed. "I could never do that. It took me all of these years just to get up enough nerve to leave home for the first time."

It was as if both women had forgotten about the bad air that had been between them when they first met.

"Don't you worry about a thing, Little Sister. You'll be fine. You got to start somewhere. Little steps lead to big steps. Remember that, Jenny Bryan. It's always scary when you step out and do something new. Don't you worry about that. Just remember to step. That's the most important thing." Trina started up the car. But before she moved it she handed Jenny one of the bags from the back seat. "Do white folks in Stone Creek eat catfish?"

Jenny could smell the hot fish in her hands. It was hard not to let on how hungry she was.

"Oh, you do, do you? You mean to tell me that Stone Creek got something in common with old Luketown? Well, I declare. I wasn't sure, but I sent James Jr. to the store for some anyway. All I know is no human being can come to Luketown and not have some of Mr. Ben's catfish. Once you have some fish you'll be going back to Stone Creek talking about how a black man named Mr. Ben and his fish sandwich saved your life." Jenny suddenly noticed that Trina had taken her glasses off. She could see that she had laughing brown eyes just like the lady who had stood waving in the doorway at her.

After taking a quick bite of her sandwich Trina Sims turned the car away from Luketown, U.S.A. She blew the horn two long times before she was out of sight and then whispered like there was still one more secret to tell. "That's how we say good-bye in Luketown, Jenny Bryan. The first one says, 'all right now, I'm going on,' and the second one says, 'Don't worry, I'll be back.'"

Trina looked over at her passenger, who wasn't really listening, who was instead biting down hard on her top lip and a million miles away in thought. "Trina, you know what? Right before I left Stone Creek, we had a big meeting in town. I didn't think much about it then. We always have a lot of meetings. But it sure is on my mind now."

"Why you thinking about some old meeting when there's all this catfish to get to know?"

"Because sometimes you have to get away from things in order to see them clear as a bell. I guess because you don't always know when you are going to see something for what it really is." Jenny looked at Trina. "Does that make any sense to you?"

"Makes plenty sense."

Jenny was talking now, talking strong and clear like Trina had not heard her talk before. She kept talking. "Sometimes when you live in a small place everybody thinks they have to say and do just like everybody else. In a little place like Stone Creek it's really scary to give birth to your own thinking. People can be so mean sometimes if you disagree with them. It's already so lonely way out there in the country. And it can get even worse if you think of things for yourself. Most people I know don't want to be left standing out there by themselves. Even when they know that's the right place to be. So most folks just go along with everything, because that's what everybody else is doing."

"Jenny Bryan, girl, I don't know who is doing all that deep thinking over there, you or that catfish, but what you saying got a whole lot of truth swimming around in it."

After some moments of quiet, Jenny's nose started moving around in the air.

"I keep smelling coconut from somewhere. Do you smell it?"

"It's either Mama's hair grease or it's that coconut creme pie she sent by me for you. The Queen puts a little coconut in anything walking or sitting. She won't tell me what else she puts in the hair oil, but I know the coconut is there. I'm taking my first load to Taylorsville today to sell after I get you settled in." Trina laughed, and both of the women let the quiet settle all around the car.

"Luketown ain't no secret place, Trina, but I swear y'all got some good secrets."

"Oh, we got a few." Trina smiled. "Some of our secrets, like Mama's hair oil recipe, I think we'll just keep to ourselves. But some of the other ones, some of the ones like you saw today when you were sitting there by yourself, we don't mind you telling the folks in Stone Creek or anywhere else about.

19

Because some secrets really are meant to be told. They have to be."

The two women looked at each other and then looked away. Trina pulled back on the paved highway headed for Taylorsville, where maybe both she and Jenny were starting new lives.

Queen Ida's Hair-Doing House of Waves

Lots of black women did hair in Luketown. Most of them did it just as a favor for a girlfriend, just because they were good at it, and some did it just for fun. They would sit a sister, a niece, or some other family member down in the middle of their kitchen, in the middle of an easy Saturday, laugh, talk and just do hair.

Ida Sims, who had always been known as "Queenie," was the only one of them to own her own beauty shop. Queenie Sims was serious about the beauty business. But everybody knew she was more serious about the beauty part than the business part. She had been Luketown's first female business owner. For thirty years now, her Hair-Doing House of Waves was where the women of Luketown and a few other towns came to treat themselves when they had a few extra dollars and felt like being served by the Queen of Deep Down Beauty.

On those days when life had been just a bit too hard and the women of Luketown had taken perfect care of everybody else except themselves, they came to Queen Ida's for some relief. Usually Fridays and Saturdays, when they needed just a little extra attention, they called up the Queen and asked if she had any space in her afternoon for them. The women would walk a few doors down the street or drive from somewhere close by to sit and talk and let the Queen of Hair wash and set their blues away and turn their sweet curly naps into endless oceans of waves.

Queen Ida's Hair-Doing House of Waves might have looked like just a hole in the wall to a stranger passing through Luketown, but inside she had built a place of honor for black women and their many different kinds of hair. She had decorated her one-room shop just like something out of those old black and white movies.

Miss Ida was always saying she wanted to make the women who dropped by feel like royalty themselves. Mr. Andy from down the street had covered her two swivel chairs in purple velvet, just for added effect.

Hanging from every wall were soft spotlights, clean sparkling mirrors, and photographs of women who, Miss Ida said, were "some of the most beautiful black women ever born." And in between all the pretty pictures she had small signs printed up with what she called her "words to be beautiful by." One of her favorites was "Beauty is not something your Mama and Daddy gave you, beauty is something you must give yourself permission to have. So get to work!"

Queenie Sims believed in making her women feel like each and every one of them had finally won the black woman's lottery jackpot! She had the idea, years ago, that black women needed some special love and attention after all their years of having to take care of everybody else. So she decided to go into the business of treating them like queens every chance she got. That's how Miss Queenie got and kept her name.

Even though the sign said "Hair-Doing House of Waves," to each and every black woman who went there each week, it also became a private rest stop, vacation, hot tub, emergency room, and restaurant, all in one. Not only did their scalps benefit from Ida's homemade creams and conditioners, but the good and honest talk they got back from her helped them work out some important things they were battling in their own private lives.

When Ida Sims got through with her customers, not only did she have the women of Luketown looking good, but she also had one or two of them thinking and believing something good about themselves as well. Her beauty shop wasn't just about fixing up what was on top of the head, it was also about cleaning out the years of dust hidden inside the deep corners of their lives.

After every head had been brushed and styled, and before anybody ever thought about leaving, she offered each customer a cup of tea as well as a slice of homemade coconut creme pie. And each customer who stood up to leave always got a little surprise box of something. A gift wrapped up in leftover Christmas paper. Something sweet secretly tucked down in their handbags with a little note attached. With that kind of special attention, no wonder Ida Sims had been in business thirty years. There were other shops in other towns nearby, but no one had ever opened up another beauty shop in Luketown to compete with the Hair-Doing House of Waves.

Ida Sims worked three shifts a day with two customers at a time. Each shift lasted about two hours, depending on the length and thickness of the hair. But as busy as she was, she never thought about getting a bigger place or hiring on more help. She said she could only give quality care to the hair and heads of two women at a time and no more than six per day.

Quality was more important to Queenie Sims than making more money.

Women who came to Queen Ida's were never sure who would come in at the same time. They never knew which two would arrive and sit side by side for at least two hours with only each other as company. Some of them might have been friends before, but some others might never have spoken to each other before that day. That was part of the beauty of Ida's place, never being sure of just who you might be getting your hair done beside.

Miss Ida always believed that they would talk and by the end of the day make friends with each other. And because of that, they would have more to share the next time they saw each other out in the world doing something else.

There was no waiting room in the House of Waves. There was no room for anybody to avoid somebody else's eyes. There were no magazines, and it was rare to hear any music. It was Queen Ida's mission to get people to talk to each other. The rest of that stuff, Ida said, "you can do anytime." This was the sacred beauty hour.

Her grandmother told her way back when she first started her business to always remember that there were some black women who never got the free time that other women got in their lives to make and keep friends. These were the black women who for all their time on earth had worked two and three jobs. These women had taken care of their own children and somebody else's too. Ida Sims decided way back then that bringing black women together to be friends was an important part of her all-round beauty work. This was where she started making the women of Luketown pay attention to their inside beauty.

No matter what day it was and no matter which two customers came in, there was always a lively conversation going on inside the House of Waves. In this relaxed time of working and talking, a lot more than hair-doing went on. In fact, nine times out of ten, somebody stood up to leave with a new, five-dollar hairdo and a million-dollar attitude. Queen Ida softly preached that creating outside beauty only lasted a week but inside beauty lasted for as long as the head itself stayed around.

Arizona Scott was in the food service business. She was a cook, and had been for all her adult life, at a little eating place on the edge of town called the Hambone Grill. She spent her days leaning over hot stoves and heating ovens. Wearing a hair net was usually the fanciest thing that ever happened to her hair.

Arizona came over every Friday after lunch for Ida's hot mint-oil treatment. She came for the scalp massage with the peppermint shampoo, then the coconut oil massaged in by big handfuls. She also came for the one-on-one attention that the Queen and the Queen's brush would always give her.

Arizona had always liked getting her hair brushed as a child. But she was forced to grow up quick and leave her girlhood behind when she had her first baby at 15. With everything there was to do, taking care of the baby and checking in on her mama as well as working full time, there was no time left to do something simple like take a brush to her own hair. There was only time to brush other people's hair every day. So when Arizona came to Queen Ida's, it was really for some attention.

Arizona was 10 years younger than Queenie Sims and 20 younger than Mae Bennett, the well-dressed principal of the local high school who had also just arrived for her monthly perm touch-up.

Mae Bennett was an old-time hell-raiser. She was Queenie's best and worst customer. She was always there and always giving her grief. Mae had traveled all around the world and owned more clothes than the local department store.

White folks pretty much hated Mae because she was always in their faces about something. She never said anything nice and gentle. She said it just like she felt it. She was usually right about what she said, but white folks never liked her tone or her attitude much. So they had done everything in their power to make her life miserable and had tried for years to run her out of the state. She could have made a lot more money somewhere else. But she didn't want to give them the satisfaction, so she had never left.

But these days all the fighting was catching up with her inside and outside health. Her short hair was breaking off by the combful. Queenie had seen and heard that poison swirling around in Mae Bennett's body for years. With every visit it meant there was still hope she still might let go of all that poison one day.

Mae Bennett had put on a towel to protect her purple silk dress and was just now going under the dryer wearing her ten-minute conditioner cap. Arizona heard the dryer come on just as Queen Ida's fingers began to massage the peppermint shampoo deep into her wet hair. Arizona's eyes closed and her head fell backward, relaxed, half on the wash board and half in the sink.

"I said it once and I'll say it a thousand times, that white girl is running from something." Mae Bennett's voice spilled out from underneath the hot air of the dryer. "I ain't never run from nothing or no one in my life, but I tell you what, I know running when I see it."

"Hey, excuse me, Miss Lady!! How come I don't hear y'all thinking good beauty shop thoughts out loud this morning? That's what I want to know. Don't you start that evil air-swirling in here, Mae Bennett. You know my rules. It's about beauty outside and in. Arizona, do you hear me?" The Queen was pointing to everybody in the tiny room. Arizona smiled twice as big as normal and shook her head quickly.

"But, come on now, let me ask y'all this," Arizona said. "What if it's not some*thing* she's running from but some*one*? Hmmmm?" She lifted her head up too far from Queenie's hands, and Ida gently pushed Arizona's soapy head back down onto the washboard, pushing and pulling each strand of hair around every bubble, trying not to listen.

"Girl, I told you, you cannot have a hard head and a beautiful head at the same time. It's humanly impossible. So be still." Queenie picked up the hand sprayer and tested the water to make sure it was warm. Then she whispered down to her customer as she pulled her hair gently, "Hold still, I said."

"But Trina said the girl was shaking like a leaf when she was sitting out there in the car. Why would she be so scared of little old us?" Arizona wondered.

"Close your eyes, Arizona. It's time to rinse."

"Already?" Arizona stuck out her lips and closed her eyes. "Ooohhhh, Miss Ida, do you know how good that peppermint feels cutting through this week's worth of double cheeseburger grease? Come on now, let it stay up there a little longer. We on the black woman's clock now."

Queenie laughed quietly to herself. She didn't like to talk too loud when she was shampooing heads. That was usually when she went to humming something. But Mae Bennett was in today, and she knew she would have to be on guard so that Arizona wouldn't pick up too much of Mae's everyday meanness and leave with it tucked somewhere under her arm. Arizona had a good spirit even though she had had to fight her way through high school. They always teased her about being dark-skinned with curly "good" hair. Queenie knew the only quiet time she would get with Arizona would be while Mae was under the dryer, so she tried to get Arizona to relax right away.

"So, Arizona, tell me about your week, Girl. Tell me how everything went."

"Oh, come on, Queenie. I want to talk gossip about Trina and that white girl she picked up at the train station. That's more exciting than any slow, pork-chop-smelling week. Come on now, tell me what you really think." Queenie could tell it was too late. Mae's question had already gotten inside of Arizona's peacefulness. For the rest of the morning Arizona was not going to leave it alone.

Arizona looked at Queenie. "Miss Ida, you been so quiet. You ain't said a word about nothing since they left here, and that was over half an hour ago."

"What . . . what did you say, Arizona? Girl, I can't hear you from way over here." Mae Bennett was squirming like a snake underneath the dryer. "I see your mouth moving, but I can't hear you. Queenie, I swear, you put me under the loudest dryer of all." Arizona and Queenie looked at each other and couldn't help but laugh out loud at how nosy Mae Bennett was being.

"Mae Bennett, what you talking about? That's the only dryer I got."

"What? Say what?" Mae leaned out from under the hair dryer to hear what Queenie's mouth was saying.

Queenie stopped her rinsing. She leaned toward Mae, talking slow as syrup. "I said, you know good and well that's the only dryer I got."

"Oh, that's right, Girl. I forgot." Mae waved her hand in the air at her. "All this money I been paying you all these years made me forget you still only got one hair dryer. I swear I don't know where all my money is going. Ha!" Mae laughed out loud. Queenie cut her an eye and mumbled something up under her breath. Arizona sat there smiling and watching the show between these two old friends.

Mae Bennett was not finished. "Queenie," she said, "I swear, you got to get another one. We need one of those quiet dryers in this place. We need one like the white women have over in their place. Because I need to be able to hear what's being said at all times, just to make sure that it's coming out correct. It's just the old school teacher in me. I need to be able to hear myself talk, even when I'm sitting in this chair conditioning my hair. And more important, I need to be able to hear what *y'all* have to say back to me about what I said, just so we can keep the good fight going strong." Mae's private laugh threw her back into her dryer chair.

Queenie Sims's back got straight as a board. Her hands flew up like a stop sign. "There will never be a fight in here, Mae Bennett. Not in here. Never. The big old world makes us fight each other everywhere else—but not in here. Are you listening to me? Not while I live and breathe."

"Oh, Girl, you know I'm just playing. Now you know that a new hair dryer is not too much to ask for. So go on now, Queenie. Do right by your best customer and take care of that before I come back next week, okay?" Mae stuck her fingers up under her cap and poked around to see what was going on up there.

She kept half talking to herself and half to the whole room. "I tell you the truth; they can send a man up to the moon, but they can't make a special hair dryer just for black women's beauty shop time. If I told y'all once I told y'all a thousand times, don't *nobody* care about the overall, general social improvement of the black woman on this here earth. Now this is just one more thing that proves it to me." Mae leaned back looking up under the loud hot dryer and kept on talking to herself, while still threatening the life of the dryer.

Arizona opened her eyes and looked up at Queenie Sims. "Miss Queenie, come on, I know you got to be thinking *some*thing?"

"Oh, I don't know, Arizona. I guess I was thinking about Trina. Seeing her today was a good surprise. She's been under so much pressure lately. I can just tell. She is really wound up tight." Queenie shook her head the way she did whenever she was real sure about something. "I'm real worried about her."

Mae leaned forward, coming out from under the dryer again as if she heard her name called. "And if I said it once, I said it a million times, all that little girl of yours needs is a little roll in the hay with the right man and she'll be fine. That girl spends too much time by herself. I tell you, it's just not healthy. She just does not have enough fun in her life. She's still a growing girl, just like me. And don't ask me how I know what I know about what is and is not fun. I just do. So there! And if you say I said it, I'll say you lying through your teeth. Ain't no tape recorder hidden up under this old dinosaur machine, is it?" Mae leaned back looking under the dryer and laughing to herself.

"All right, Mae Bennett. Watch yourself!" Queenie shouted. All three of them were laughing when Arizona whispered to Queen Ida, "I see she can hear what she wants to, when she wants to, from up under that dryer."

Queenie nodded in agreement and then got serious again. "Trina's smoking more and more. Every time I see her she's lighting up another one. I wanna say something about it, but she won't never talk about it, not with me."

Things settled back down and Queenie finished wringing all

the water out of Arizona's grease-free hair. "So, Queenie, what you think she's so wound up about?"

"Everything! You name it, and that baby girl of mine will worry about it. She's been that way since she was a little girl. She don't need to ever be nobody's mama because she already tries too hard to mama the world. And now, with her quitting her good job and me and her trying this new business thing, Lord have mercy. I just don't know. I knew it was trouble when she started wearing those dark sunglasses again, the ones her crazy brother gave her to go along with that fast car. But she's always been like that, almost too sensitive. You know what I mean? Trina feels she's got to save everybody's life that she can. That's too much for anybody to hold onto."

Arizona patted her fingers on Queenie's arm, trying to calm her nerves back down. The power cut off on the dryer, and Mae stood up and stretched like a polar bear. She let out a loud yawn and, while holding her backside like it was aching from sitting so long, walked over to the other two women.

"Queenie Sims, I'm gonna sue you."

"Now what did I do?"

"I think this plastic cap has melted into my poor tender head. I think you gonna have to shave it all off and start over with some Miracle Grow." The three women howled out in a chorus together.

"Girl, sit down and tell me about your beautiful week." Mae dropped down into the empty chair next to them, out of breath.

Arizona had another question. "Well, now, here's what I really need to understand. Why, Miss Queenie, did Trina bring that girl by here? Just before they came in you had just said Trina was supposed to stop by tomorrow and pick up that hair oil."

"I'm not clear about it myself, Arizona. All I know is my Trina wouldn't do nothing without a reason."

"Oh, come on now, Girls. Since you didn't ask me, I'll tell you why. She came by here because white people are the crookedest creatures on the earth. And that white girl probably told that good-hearted Trina she had to go pee or something and Trina just brought her on home 'cause that's just how Trina was raised." Mae Bennett stretched all the way back in the purple velvet chair and let out a loud laugh. But Queenie was on her quick and fast.

"Mae, you are just never gonna change your stripes, are you? There you go again, talking about something that you don't know nothing about. And even if what you say was true, even if Jenny did have to go to the bathroom, then why did she come all this way out here only to sit out in the car?"

"I'll tell you why. Because when she got here and saw this little, iddy-biddy one-room place of business of yours, she thought she might catch a disease or something. So she just up and changed her mind rather than come inside. That's what white folks do all the time. They always changing their mind. Always. They tell you one thing one minute, and then change it to something else. They change it to whatever they need to change it to. I tell you, they make me sick."

33

"Oh, Mae, come on now! Long as I have known you, and that has been a long time, you have always had the worst of things to say about white folks. I am not gonna let you start back in on the evils of white people today, not today. No, Ma'am. I have been trying to get you to think something different for 20 years, and nothing has worked so far. But it's just too early in the morning for all that meanness. Look outside at all that sunshine coming down, free of charge, if you need a reminder."

"I'm reminded all right, Queenie, that white folks are truly the worst people of all times." Mae Bennett clapped her hands together as she said what she said.

Arizona got quiet. She was thinking about what Mae was saying. "Queenie, Trina did say Jenny was scared."

"Arizona, don't bite into what Mae is trying to feed you. A person ain't bad just because they scared."

Queenie was wiping her hands off. She had finished putting the conditioner on Arizona's hair and moved her down a chair to the window in the sun. Arizona's hair took the heat of the sun better than the hair dryer. She would sit there a while and let her hair drink in all the coconut juice it wanted.

Queenie went on. "Trina also said she hadn't never been around no real black folks. Give the girl a chance."

Mae got up and walked toward Queenie's high wash chair and sat down right where Arizona had been sitting. It was her turn to speak. "I'm glad she was scared myself. Because as long as they are scared of you, then they'll leave you alone."

Queenie turned toward her oldest customer. "Mae, as long as people are scared of each other, ain't nothing ever gonna change. They gonna keep acting ugly toward us, and we gonna keep acting ugly toward them. And they are gonna keep living over there. And we are gonna keep living over here. And we are going to keep lying to ourselves, saying we believe in brotherhood just because we were always too scared to say out loud 'I'm scared of everybody who ain't like me.'"

Mae Bennett smoothed out her skirt. "Well, I don't know about you, but I don't live here because I'm scared. I have lived here for 50 years because I feel safe here, because this is my home. Because I don't have to look over my shoulder when I walk around and hold my eyes straight like a gun at anybody. I don't ever want to live somewhere like Stone Creek where I know I am not wanted. So they can stay all-white if they want to, for all I care. If I see one of them coming this way, I tell you this, I'm going home to get my gun too."

Arizona and Queenie stopped what they were doing, turned, and both stared at Mae Bennett. They looked at her like she had changed shape and voice and color and everything, all because of one word. They looked at her like she had suddenly become someone they had never met or seen before.

"Everybody thinking that that's the cure for everything. Everybody reaching for their gun, Mae Bennett. Used to be we reach for somebody's hand to shake, now we reach for a gun to point. Everybody putting up signs all over the place saying 'Come on in, your gun is welcome here.' And anybody who does that, as far as I'm concerned, has given up and don't believe in nothing good no more. And from what I hear you saying, you stooping right down there in the pig pen with the rest of them."

After a while Arizona lay her head back in the sun like she just didn't know what to say to anybody, like she was just tired. But she was the one who finally broke the silence that was heavy in the air.

"Even if you didn't really want to, Miss Queenie, wouldn't you still like to know that you *could* live anywhere in the world, if you had the money and if you wanted to?" Arizona's eyes were closed as she talked. It was almost like she was dreaming the way her voice sounded.

Mae didn't give Queen Ida a chance to answer Arizona. "You might be a black woman, and it might almost be the year 2000. But what does what you said really mean? I'll tell you what that means. It means the same thing it did in 1800. Nothing. This world for black women hasn't changed from then to now. And they will never let you forget that. Never. And what I'm talking about they won't print in *Essence* magazine. You need to open your eyes, stop dreaming, and stop fooling yourself. There are people who work extra hard so that you will never climb out of your black woman's place and do anything else with your life but flip hamburgers at the Hambone Grill, just like you are doing."Arizona's face fell down like a rock in water.

"Mae Bennett!" Queenie spun her around in the chair and the two women were suddenly eye to eye, staring at each other. "That ain't true. I don't believe none of what you saying. And don't talk to Arizona like that. You might as well take a gun and shoot all the dreams of every black woman that ever was, when you say things like that. You got proof of what you saying? Don't you dare put Arizona down like that!"

"My life is all the proof I need."

Queenie Sims's back got straight as a board. "Mae, you know the rules. Look around you if you need a reminder. I don't allow that kind of talk in my shop. You know that. That ain't nothing but talk from a dead woman for sure. You are getting too wound up inside, too wound up for anything that I'm doing on your head to be of any good to you. No good at all. And you getting everybody else upset too."

Mae turned and stared at the wall. The sign in front of her read, in oversize letters, "When you change your thoughts, you change your words, then you change yourself." With nowhere else to go in the room, she just closed her eyes altogether.

Queenie gently moved out of Mae's face. She turned the chair back around and put her hands back on her shoulders. She eased Mae Bennett's head back into the wash tray. She tested the water and began rinsing the cream out of her dyed jet-black hair. When all of the suds had been washed away, she took her fingers and held up to the sunlight different pieces of the short uneven hair.

"Mae, see here, just look at this. I told you last time how your hair is showing the wear and tear of all that hate you got inside of you. Look at this, Mae. Just look at all of this damaged hair. This is not good, Mae Frances Bennett. This is not good at all. I told you about it, but you didn't believe me."

"Queenie," Mae was trying to get a word in, but it was no use.

"Mae, I know you still don't believe me. But what you spend your time worrying and thinking about every day is just as harmful or just as helpful as the food you eat every day. Your hair is brittle and breaking off bad, and there's nothing I can do about it. You just keep your money and don't come here if you're not gonna do your part. Because no amount of washing and lotion is gonna help when all the damage is moving from the inside out."

Mae Bennett had her hands up in a fighting position. "And I believe I told you, Queenie Sims, that the people who raised me used to say that there was bad hate and good hate, and good hate was good for you. It'll make you strong. I still believe that."

Arizona raised her head up out of the sun like she had felt a bad ghost come into the room all of a sudden. Everything in the beauty shop got warm quick. "I'm sorry, Miss Bennett, I don't mean no harm. I've known you since I was a little girl growing up around here. I've looked up to you because of all the things you have done. But what you just said, I know that's not true. It just can't be true. Hate has got to be the worst poison there is. I seen how it can walk on your rooftops all sneaky and drop down in the middle of your house without being announced. I seen how it can burn things down in a minute. Just look how long it's been around us. Look where it's got us today, all around the world fighting each other like we crazy."

"That's the truth, Arizona. That's the gospel truth." Queenie's voice was quiet and low.

Before Queenie could put a towel around her head, Mae Bennett had flown out of the big purple chair and was standing in the middle of the tiny floor. Flinging and dripping water everywhere and pointing with both hands like pistols, she was screaming at the top of her lungs. Queenie and Arizona could only stare at her and wonder who this strange woman was, popping out of an old familiar body.

"I tell you what, I have just about had enough of this for one day! No, I have had enough of this forever." She spun around and kept talking. "One of you is telling me my hair is falling out, while the other one is telling me who I need to love and what I cannot hate. Well, I don't need or deserve this from either one of you!"

Mae pointed at Arizona first. "Arizona, you ain't dry behind the ears yet, so I don't have nothing else to say to you. But Queenie, I'm just sick to death of all this be-kind-to-white-folks talk you been pouring in my ears for years now. I tell you I have had it up to here." Her hand tapped hard on the top of her head. "I am too old to be told week after week that I need to let go of my hate. I'll have you know that my hate has kept my mind alert and probably my old heart beating. My hate is a friend of mine!"

Queenie dropped her head and wiped her hands on her apron and looked tired all of a sudden. Mae Bennett was turning into a woman she had never laid eyes on before, right before their eyes. All of the pain and hurt had finally boiled up into somebody Queenie just didn't recognize.

"And one more thing, Queenie Sims. Before you go stepping out into the world with your new little black woman's business, you better realize that everybody is gonna be against you right from the start. Because if you just working on colored women's hair then don't nobody care about that. But the minute you start trying to compete with white folks for something, something far more daring and reaching that makes a lot more money and makes you better known, then you gonna get it from white folks the most, but black folks gonna hate you too. You mark my word. You'll see."

Queenie couldn't believe her ears. "Mae Bennett, you look over here in the mirror at yourself. Because you need to really see what you look like saying something like that to me."

Mae Bennett was beyond listening now. She was pointing everywhere now, just like she was in some kind of meeting, reading from a list and checking off items one by one. "Not you or you," her finger went first to Arizona then to Queenie, "know what I been through in my life when it comes to white folks and pain. I have seen too much and have been through too many fires. Don't you dare try to tell me what I'm supposed to feel."

Mae Bennett put her hands on her hips and walked a few steps before she turned back around. "I don't know why I keep coming back here week after week. There's a place over in New City where I could go just as easy, where I don't have to get a sermon before I get my hair done. This is it for me, Sisters. I will never step foot in this place again. Never. "

"Don't say that, Mae. Don't say that. It's been 20 years. We been together a long time, and you know I can't let you back in here if you say that and leave here like this. Don't say that if you don't mean it."

"I mean it, Queenie, and I promise I'll keep myself true to it." Mae Bennett reached out and picked up the hot comb that was sitting there, smoking and ready to be used. She reached back and threw it as hard as she could right at the same mirror Queenie had wanted her to look into. The mirror cracked right in the middle, and the broken pieces fell hard to the floor. Queenie screamed. Arizona ran to the corner. Mae tore off her plastic apron. She grabbed her purse and smoothed out her dress.

"Mae Bennett, don't you walk out that door. If you walk out that door like this, you know what that means." Queenie had her hand on her hips now. Arizona was standing up, looking almost afraid but not saying a word.

Mae threw on the floor the surprise gift box Queenie had stuck down in her purse while she was under the dryer. She slapped a 10-dollar bill down on the counter. "Y'all sisters keep the change, you hear me. 'Cause Mae Bennett don't need nobody."

Mae stormed out the front of the shop with the House of Waves towel still pinned around her shoulders. She never stopped to close the door or say good-bye. When she was halfway down the street and realized she was still wearing the towel, she tore it off and stomped on it, out in the middle of the hard dirt street.

The warm morning air pushed in and moved around the tiny room. It stopped first at Arizona and then moved to Queenie, who had folded herself down in her own velvet wash chair now. Her face was streaming with tears, and it wanted more than anything to just fall on down into her hands and not move for a long, long time. She knew one of the oldest friendships she ever had was laying out in the middle of the road somewhere, and she didn't know if it would ever be picked up and saved.

The next morning when Queenie took her key out to open up her beauty shop, there was a small flat box waiting on the steps with her name on it. She put her bags down and decided to open it up right there. The morning was cool, and she still had a little time. It wasn't seven o'clock yet, and her first two customers weren't due until eight.

She unwrapped the paper, which she recognized as some of her own from two Christmases ago. She took the top off the box. In it was a small framed picture that she had never seen of herself. It was a picture someone had taken from the side when she wasn't looking. She didn't remember the day or the time when it could have been taken. She didn't even know who could have snapped it. Queenie was smiling in the picture. She was smiling wide and pretty and big. She was dressed up and looking beautiful, and she had on sunglasses too. Sunglasses that made her suddenly see her daughter Trina's face deep in the lines of her own.

The picture made Queenie smile. She hated taking pictures, everybody knew that. So whoever had taken this one knew when to take it, right when she was looking the other way. The frame around the picture was handmade out of dark cherry wood and a large box of purple velvet was the whole wide background. It looked like the exact same purple velvet that Mr. Andy had covered Queenie's chairs in. Queenie stared at it with her mouth open.

On the back of the card she read, "You have always put your heart on the line for us. I just thought it was time to put yourself on the wall too. Thanks to you I'm feeling mighty beautiful today. Just wanted you to know. Do you have an opening for next week? Love, Arizona."

Queenie picked up the torn pieces of paper and tape and put them in her pocket. She put the key in the door and flipped on the light. She stood in the doorway for a minute, looking around at the tiny room that sometimes just plain seemed bigger than it was. She looked up on her walls, into all the smiling faces of black women that covered the walls of her shop like some kind of beautiful wallpaper. She put her things down and didn't bother to close the door. The Hair-Doing House of Waves was open for business.

The Church of the Holy Whiteness

The old one-room church sat out in the middle of the woods, away from Stone Creek and everything else in the whole wide world. It was the oldest building in that part of the state. On one of its eight sturdy legs a large smooth brick read "Built in 1839."

The Church of the Holy Whiteness had stood there for more than 150 years. It was old, but it did not look or smell or seem old. In many ways it looked better than any new building around, and it was certainly better kept. Some part of it was always being worked on or cared for by a church member. But more than any other kind of care it got, it was always being painted. Twice a year were planned painting days. Nothing was more important than keeping the old church perfectly white.

Everything about the Church of the Holy Whiteness was white. The color of the church and the color of all the people who worshipped there were the same. The steps leading up to it were perfectly white. The chimney, the window panes, the doorknobs, even the nails, before they used them, had been dipped in the whitest of paint and touched up after being hammered in. Keeping the church white, inside and out, was something the members held more than dear.

There were no roads that led up to the old church. There never had been a road, not in all its long history. People parked their cars and trucks down on Old State Highway 24 and walked up a half a mile through the woods. Every year the town voted whether or not to cut a road up to the church, but every year most of the townsfolk voted no. They continued to believe that getting to the old church should never be something that was easy to do. That's how it had always been done. That's how it was still done. The citizens of Stone Creek didn't like changes.

The other churches in town were mainly used on Sundays only, but not the Church of the Holy Whiteness. This church was really part church and part meeting hall. It was part church and part school. Even though it was the hardest church of all to get to, it was also the place that meant the most to the people who lived there.

When you entered the front of the Church of the Holy Whiteness there was an old sign that read "Do Right" and nothing more. When you left through the back of the church, there was another sign that read the exact same thing. This was where the great grandmothers and the great grandfathers of the citizens of Stone Creek had been born, baptized, and raised. This was where the first town laws had been written and voted on. This was where they had first dreamed and planned their futures. This one big room with 500 seats was where their children still came two nights a week to learn the same old, all-white ways of Stone Creek. And this had been where, in 1907, Stone Creek citizens first brought, by mob force, the last 19 brown men and women who lived in the county.

To the old church they were brought and dumped, with their hands and feet tied together. They were made to sit in the middle of the floor like a pile of useless things pulled from the river. And on the following day, from sunrise to sunset, one after the other of Stone Creek's citizens came forward and stood in the pulpit to preach something to the captive listeners about the old, perfect gospel of the holy whiteness. Everything they said that day was about the goodness of white things and people and the evilness of black and colored things and people. For one whole day, nonstop, they read sermons and sang to these, the last people of color living in their county.

These were black folks whose grandmothers and grandfathers had decided after the war was over in 1865 to settle around Stone Creek, Kentucky. These were free folk with their minds and hearts on freedom. They had stopped and built cabins all along the Creek because of the long, clear farmland and the clear, fresh spring water. These God-fearing people had stopped there to build homes and try to plow out a decent living for themselves and their families. These hardworking people of deep faith didn't know there would be as much hate walking on top of this rich land as there was clear spring water running below it, but there was.

Almost one hundred years ago, on one day, from sunrise to sunset, 19 good human beings lay piled in the middle of the floor of the oldest church in the county. These free folk had seen hate before in their lives, but the evilness that swirled around them on this day was as big as the sun in the sky, and they were very afraid. The Citizens Council of Stone Creek kept them there until they were finished with their prayers and sermons and fiery speeches. The same Citizens Council then walked them down to the town square, drew a starting line in the dirt, and gave them to the count of five to run for their lives.

The same church members shot many of them through their backs as they ran for freedom and the county line. From then on Stone Creek would be known as the only all-white town left in Kentucky.

That had been way back in 1907, but no black or colored folks had ever lived in Stone Creek again. Now, ninety years later, a special town meeting had been called at the Church of the Holy Whiteness. The townspeople were hurrying toward it from every direction. They had left their cars and trucks somewhere below them and were walking up the rest of the way. Some of them walked in groups like families. Some of them came alone. The men and boys were dressed mostly in grays and browns, with a little blue here and there. The women and girls all had on skirts and dresses of softer colors.

When they reached the front door, the men took off their hats. As they entered, all of them walked past the "Do Right" sign. Some of the older people even reached out to touch it, as if it had some kind of special power. Then they all took their regular seats on one of the old wooden benches in the open room. The same seats where they sat every Sunday. Maybe where they had sat as children.

This was Wednesday, their second Wednesday meeting that month. The old church was buzzing with voices and whispering.

"All right, all right! Let's please have a little come-to-order silence if you don't mind." The shortest man sitting in the first row of chairs that were turned and facing the church stood to speak. He was Jack Murphy, and he hit his hand against the wooden table like it was a hammer. The crowd turned their loud talking to whispers and soon all their voices died down into a sea of silence.

"As many of you believers already know, there is a situation that has been going on over the last few weeks. This situation is located just about five miles from here, off of Old Highway 24. Some of us believe it concerns all of us here in Stone Creek. And then again some of us believe it don't concern us at all. But there was enough who feel that it does for us to call another meeting for tonight. We need to talk about all this and get it out in the open so we can go on to other things. Let's try to get everything said and then make some good decisions and get back down the hill. Most of us got to go to work early in the morning."

A sudden voice rang out from the very back of the room. "I say no more talking, damn it. Let's go do something about it. And I say let's do it the old way. I still have my granddaddy's old shotgun in the barn. I say let's use what we got to get rid of it. And I say let's do it tonight." Some of the other men's voices followed this single loud one out into the middle of the room in agreement.

"All right, Nate, let's just hold off on all that if you don't mind. Let's keep to our rules of respect for each other when we come to meet together. I know our feelings may be a bit on edge about this, but there's a lot to talk about tonight." The man turned from speaking to just one person in the crowd and tried to address everybody. "Like I was saying, if you been listening to all the gossip, you might have missed the facts of what's been going on here. Before we go on maybe I better take a minute to put all the facts on the table."

Jack Murphy was the mayor of Stone Creek. He had only been elected a few months before. He was the first Stone Creek mayor who had not been born there. He didn't win by much, but he had won fair and square, so the citizens were willing to give him a chance. But this meeting was his first real test. Jack Murphy walked from behind the table with his hands deep in his pants pockets.

"Just about a month ago Fred Reese was out hunting over by the water tower on some of that land that nobody hardly goes to anymore, when he saw some colored men on what he thought was Stone Creek land. He said he stopped and watched them for a while." Murphy chewed on his tongue a little and then went on. "He said they looked like they were hammering something down in the ground. He said he decided to get a little closer and take a better look."

Jack Murphy stopped talking and blew his nose in his pocket handkerchief. It got so quiet you could hear a pin drop. He went on telling his story. "Fred walked up a little closer and got behind one of those big oak trees up there and listened in for a while. That's when he saw the brand new building standing up there behind some trees. Fred said he saw the new church standing up there plain as day."

As Murphy finished his story up, the crowd of church members mumbled under their breaths to each other. The people in the old building kept watching Stone Creek's newest mayor go over the story they had heard told a hundred different ways over the last few weeks.

49

"Come on, Jack, get to it. We been waiting on this for what seems like forever. We all know what's sitting up there. We just need to decide what we gonna do about it. I don't know about the rest of you. But as long as I live, I ain't living with or beside no coons. My daddy never did, and neither did his daddy, and I ain't neither."

Buck Jones hadn't voted for Jack Murphy. Even though Murphy had lived in Stone Creek since he was five years old, Buck considered him an outsider and didn't want him to have the job. Buck Jones thought Jack Murphy talked too much. He told everybody that he believed a good hard day's work would kill Murphy dead.

Buck was one of the richest men around. He owned the county's only farm chemical plant over on Red Road. He made plant fertilizers and animal feed. Buck was bound and determined to push Jack Murphy to the limit. He had come to the meeting with his three grandsons, Jimmy Jr., Freddie, and Luke, who were sitting quietly by his side. He believed in teaching the children of Stone Creek by action and not by cheap talk.

Murphy turned back to keep talking to the crowd. "Well, it seems as if the colored folks of Silver, Kentucky, which sits right next door to Stone Creek, those ones from Great John the Baptist, outgrew their old church and started this new building project. Old Great John the Baptist was started about 10 years after this church, for those of you who don't know, so its been around a long time."

Buck Jones jumped up from his seat. "Hey! Just what is this, a Black Power fund-raiser or a Stone Creek town meeting? I can't tell the difference no more." Buck Jones was waving his arms. The rest of the crowd stirred and grumbled along with him.

"Look, Buck, it's my job to give all the facts. That's all I'm trying to do. Those people have built a new church, and they built it fast. It's big and it's new, and soon there will be colored people in that church. Maybe a lot of colored people. I don't know. I think it's important to look at how long this church and those folks have been around. That tells you a lot about how they might fight to keep it. That's all. I just think you make better decisions about things when you know the whole story. That's all I'm trying to do."

A voice yelled out, "Just where'd they get the money for something big and new like that?"

"Probably stole it," another voice answered back while the crowd laughed.

"Is it on Stone Creek land or not? That's all I want to know," a woman holding her two young boys in her lap asked softly.

"Please, folks. We'll get to all your questions, but hear me out, please." Murphy had his hands back in the air. "Martha Sue was able to find out some things from the land office over there in Silver, and the information was verified by our own office. Exactly where the stakes are in the ground is *not* on our property. I repeat, it is *not* on Stone Creek land. Did everybody hear me?"

The whole church buzzed. Some of the men turned to talk to others sitting next to them. They whispered and some of them even started shaking hands, wiping their eyebrows and fanning with their hats.

"But," Jack Murphy continued, "I got to tell you folks, it is mighty close. My office has checked and double checked, and I got to tell you, everything has been done real legal and by the books. But where their line ends and ours begins is mighty, mighty close. And I'll tell you what, that's why we are all here tonight. Because we need to talk about what them being there means for us and for our town. We need to talk about and get it out and listen to how people are feeling about it." The men who had relaxed came back to the edge of their seats, and their mumbling got louder.

Buck Jones had been standing by where his grandsons were sitting quietly. He began to walk slowly to the front with his hands in his pocket. "Just how close is it, Mr. Mayor?"

A man who was sitting alone on the other side of the church stood up. "What does it matter if it's 50 feet or 500 or 5,000? Y'all are missing the whole point. The point is it's a nigger church, and if I'm standing anywhere in Stone Creek and can see or smell it, then it's too close. Maybe not by nobody else's law but by the first law—old Stone Creek law."

Some of the children giggled when he said the word "nigger," but he kept talking.

"It's too close. I tell you it's just too close. Now, I thought we were coming here tonight to decide just what we're gonna do about it. And then we need to just walk out of here and do it. Tonight!"

"Yeahhhhh, I say let's burn it down!" A small roar from the loudest of the men went up all around. A few stood up and were waving their hats and lighting matches and letting them burn down to their fingertips and shouting as the tips of their fingers burned a little.

Buck Jones turned and faced the men who were talking about burning the church. His voice got quiet, and he spoke his words like each one mattered. "Quiet down, boys, and blow out your fire sticks. We have to do something, but it ain't fire. These are colored folks. They'll just see fire as some kinda sign from God. They'll just build it back bigger and better than it was. Burning down is what Mama and Daddy did way back when. That's the old way. We got bigger and better ways now. Do you understand? It's got to hurt deeper than that old way."

Many in the congregation nodded their heads like they were in a spell. "We have to find a way to break their spirits and maybe even burn their souls forever. But it can't have nothing to do with fire," Jones said.

Jack Murphy had his hands up in the air trying to get some order back into the meeting. "Buck, come on, please." Murphy was waving them all down. The quiet came back to the church after a long while. Jack Murphy looked around before he spoke.

"All y'all know I wasn't born here, but I been here a good long time. And I guess that can be seen as a good thing or a bad thing. But right now I think it's a good thing. Because I get to see some things that maybe you can't see. I hope that's a part of why you voted me in. What I *can* see is something like this getting way out of hand if we aren't careful. All I'm asking is for us to think things through before we just react. That's all I'm asking."

Elijah Hunter spoke next. "And then again, Mayor, there comes a time when we can be too careful. If we're too slow we could lose everything we done worked so hard to get all these years. Next thing you know there'll be some of them Japanese coming. Then after they come there'll be some of them Mexicans. I tell you we *can* be too careful, Jack. The world is changing quicker than you know. My little acre of land ain't as big as it used to be—nobody's is. Everybody is starting to come at us pure whites from all sides. Just watch the news if you don't believe me. I tell you its gonna be another Civil War if they keep it up."

"I understand what you're saying, Buck, and it's true. It is changing quick. But we can't just fly off the handle and do the first thing that comes to mind like Great Granddaddy might have done. Times have changed. We got to keep our heads clear and make some good decisions for ourselves and for our families. It's been a long time," Murphy ran his fingers through his silver white hair, "a real long time since we did any burning down around here. I just don't think we can afford to go back to all of that. We got a heap more to lose now than we did back then. There's more laws in place now. We just gotta be careful, that's all. Why, over in Alabama they took that meeting hall away from them Klan boys."

"To hell with their law. What about our law? What about our children too?" Judy Short stood, wanting to know.

Jack Murphy kept looking out, from one side of the church to the other side. Sometimes he folded his arms, and sometimes he just let them fall free by his side. He looked worried about what he saw in the faces of the men and women of Stone Creek. There were over 500 people there. He couldn't tell what they were thinking exactly. But Jack Murphy could feel that they weren't thinking clear or careful.

He remembered these same angry faces from a different time in his own life. A time when he had seen that same kind of anger build up in his own face, 40 years ago when they had set the last fire that he knew about. He had worked hard to get rid of the anger because it had almost destroyed him and his family. Jack Murphy had learned that nothing was worth losing your family over.

"We've built up a pretty good old town over the years. We got good schools and good businesses going on, some of you like Billy Joe Bryan and his wife, Jenny, are just starting out. Some of you been around, working hard for 50 years. More good white folks are moving in here all the time. We have to always remember the past, and we have to keep what is sacred and white, true. But we have to think things through these days before we do them, because we have a lot to lose if we make the wrong move. Do you understand what I'm saying to you?"

None of the men answered Jack Murphy right back. They were talking and leaning into each other, some chewing gum and looking into their hands. Some of the men reached out for their wives' hands, and some pulled their children down closer into their laps.

Billy Joe Bryan had his arm around the back of Jenny's chair. He stood up and walked toward the table where Jack Murphy was standing. The talking began to die down quickly as all eyes moved to him. Billy Joe was a good looking young man in his early thirties. His wife was a nurse helper up at the hospital. There weren't too many young farmers like Billy Joe left in Stone Creek. Most of the young men had left the town for better jobs in bigger cities. He was a hog man just like his daddy and his uncles. He didn't usually say much at the town meetings. And he had never come up front from the regular seats before. He was nervous and twisting his hat around in both his hands. His pipe was poking out of his shirt pocket.

"Most of y'all know me pretty good. I'm a simple man. Most times I try not to say too much. I leave all that to the preacher and the lawyer man. I try to stick to making bacon sizzle and cutting pork chops." The crowd laughed and sat back easy in their seats.

"I don't like this situation no more than the rest of you. And before I came here tonight, I was ready to just grab a stick and start swinging. But Mayor Murphy has said some real good things in the last two meetings. Me and Jenny are just getting our feet up out of the mud and starting to put a little something away. I think we ought to listen and just keep an eye on everything. Maybe even set up some neighborhood watch patrols for where our land ends and theirs begins. But most of all I just wanted to say, I think its important to keep meeting and talking just like we're doing tonight. I guess that's all I have to say."

Billy Joe started walking back to his seat. "Oh, yeah, I also want to say one more thing. We ought to wrap this up soon because I don't know about the rest of y'all with your nine-to-five jobs, but my hogs start calling me at four o'clock in the morning and they don't stop till the moon comes out."

The whole church broke into laughter as Billy Joe Bryan fell back in his seat. He took his arm and pulled his wife Jenny's head toward him and gave her a friendly little chokehold around the neck. She pulled her yellow sweater down tighter around both of her wrists. He seemed proud of what he had done and said. People were reaching over and patting him on his back. Jenny Bryan brushed her red hair back behind her ears before forcing a smile out on her pale face.

The church members started one by one clapping at what Billy Joe had said. Not all of them, but most. Then they started yelling out together, over and over again, like they were in some kind of a high school pep rally, "Ci-ti-zens Pa-trol! Ci-ti-zens Pa-trol! Ci-ti-zens Pa-trol!"

Mayor Jack Murphy walked back to the center of the floor, smiling. "Well, it seems as though most of us agree. That's real good. Thank you, Billy Joe. We might almost be through here for tonight. We don't want trouble with nobody else's law. We just want to be left alone to live like we want to live. We just want what is ours to stay ours." Most of the crowd was nodding its head in agreement. "Well, if that's so, let's call this a night."

Murphy turned to find in the crowd the man who was still not smiling. "What you say, Buck? We got a deal before we leave here tonight?"

Buck was walking back to his seat. He had been standing and listening there in the middle of the floor the whole time. "Sounds like a deal with the devil, if you ask me. But, yeah, I hear you. We got a deal. 'Course you never know about us homegrown boys. I just might have my fingers crossed or something." He smiled down into his boots, and laughter followed him all the way back to his seat. Buck slapped the knee of his oldest grandson just for good luck.

"Well, then, if we have no further business, that's what we'll do. We'll watch and wait and see what happens this next week. Anybody interested in being on the citizens patrol can sign up. There's a piece of paper going around. In case you're interested, I understand that Great John the Baptist is having their first church service this Sunday coming up."

"Tell it to the National Association of Colored People, Murphy. We ain't interested," Buck Jones yelled out.

"Just giving you all the information I got, that's all. Please let us stand and sing the church anthem, and y'all be extra careful going back down the hill tonight." Jack Murphy came from behind the collection table and reached out to catch hands with the closest members. The other members reached out to hold somebody else's hand until they all stood in a wavy circle.

The members of the Church of the Holy Whiteness didn't need to pull any books out of their place. The words to "Pure and White Is Our Faith" moved up from their bellies and out through their lips. They threw back their heads, loud with song. Their many voices carried outside the windows and entered the woods and trees all around, and soon crashed headfirst somewhere out in the dark sweet night.

A few days later, three o'clock early Saturday morning, Buck Jones drove without his headlights up to the newly built Great John the Baptist Church. Earlier in the evening he had dropped his grandsons and their bikes off at the campground. The Boy Scouts were having a weekend campout.

It had all worked out so perfectly. It was dark, and there was no moon out to help him see, but Buck had grown up around these woods. He knew them like the back of his hand. He felt his way around to the back of the new building and pushed up the window closest to the ground.

As he stepped inside the dark church, the scent of new wood and polish reached his nose. He stopped for a minute, letting his eyes adjust to the darkness. When he finally saw where he was, he walked up to where the preacher would soon stand for the very first time. He climbed over where the choir would sit on Sunday. There was a small room sitting at the top of the stage almost hidden. He pushed back the curtain to it. It was no bigger than a small bathroom. The walls were all glass, and it was filled with waist-high water. The walls sat up high and proud. It was built that way so that everybody in the church would have a clear view of the preacher and whoever was about to be baptized standing there in the water with him.

Buck Jones opened the side door to the room and smiled to himself as he looked down into the tiny pool of still water. He took his hand and dipped it down. The water was cool, still, and clear. He had been told that most Baptist churches, the black ones, especially the ones that no longer actually sat right on a river bank, always made a place for baptizing their members. To the colored, baptizing was as important as the preaching itself, he had been told.

His grandsons had told him at the dinner table the night before that Great John the Baptist had just put a baptizing pool in their new church. It was the first one ever built inside a black Baptist church in this part of Kentucky. He didn't know how they knew and didn't care. They were 12, 13, and 15 years old. He didn't know how they were always finding out things that nobody else knew. But finding out that the pool was there worked out perfect for what he knew he had to do. On Sunday morning, members of Great John the Baptist, in their first-ever service in their brand new church, were planning to baptize all of the children of the church, even those who had been baptized before.

Buck Jones unzipped his jacket pocket and pulled out a small plastic bag full of fine white powder. He put it to the side while he pulled on a pair of thin plastic gloves. He picked up the bag and looked at it. It was one of the many chemicals that his company made. The strongest one of all. It was only used for the most difficult of land-clearing jobs. Once this powder was put into the water lines and sprinkled over the woods and forests, it destroyed the roots of everything it touched. This made it easy to clear the land so that new houses could be built.

Buck Jones knew that this chemical was going to be taken

off the market. It had proven to be too dangerous. It caused too many animal deaths by mistake. But it was perfect for what he needed to do. He held the poison out over the water, sprinkling it until the plastic pack was empty. He pulled off his gloves and watched the white crystals disappear. He stepped back from the pool, and as he did, he thought he heard voices. He wasn't sure.

Buck Jones dropped down low to the floor and began crawling in the blackness to the window that he had climbed in through. He didn't know who or how many might be outside, but his hearing was sharp. Somebody was out there, and they were talking in low voices. Maybe someone had followed him. He didn't see any lights outside, but he was sure he heard one man's voice, maybe two men, maybe more.

Buck had to get out of the building and into the woods. The window was right in front of him. He peeked his head through quickly to see if he could see anything. Nothing, just the darkness. He rolled out onto the ground, staying on his knees in case he had to get out of sight quickly. Above the loud crickets and frogs he could barely hear the unknown voices, but they came through the air to him again.

Whoever it was was now somewhere at the front of the church. He decided he didn't care and didn't want to know. He just wanted to get off the church grounds and back to Stone Creek. His truck was parked down the hill behind some trees, and he ran softly back toward the woods. He smiled at the excitement of having almost been caught.

At the edge of the woods he looked back over his shoulder, just to see if he could make out where the voices had come from. Buck Jones's eye caught a sparkle of light bouncing off the fender of a bicycle that looked very familiar to him. He turned and faced the church. He leaned closer into the night wind. The bike seemed to be one of three he had bought the summer before. Buck Jones stood up straight and tall and began to run full steam toward the church. As he ran, he screamed out all his grandsons' names, one after the other.

He thought he heard the hands of his three favorite boys pushing up windows. At first the only word he could get out was "No!" Then he screamed their names, "Jimmy! Luke! Freddie! No!" He thought he heard the bodies of his three favorite boys playfully sliding like dolphins across the new church floor to their secret playing place.

"Jimmy! Luke! Freddie! No! Don't!"

Just as Buck Jones's hand reached the front door he thought he heard the water in the baptizing pool breaking under the weight of his three favorite boys—sneaking, just as they had the past two Friday nights, into the new colored baptizing pool for a final swim before the new church opened on Sunday.

Promises to Keep

Trina Sims put on her sunglasses. She knew she was driving too fast through the streets of Taylorsville, but it was Monday morning and she was late to pick up Jenny. The weekend was over. Jenny Bryan had spent it at Moore Farm, talking to Dorothy Moore about the job as house manager. Jenny was heading back to Stone Creek, and Trina couldn't remember what time she had to be at the train station.

She had spent all morning trying to work up sales for Queenie's hair oil. She had been slowed down at her last stop by a crook of a store manager who wasn't interested in business but in playing games. Weeks ago Trina and the owner of Your Neighborhood Market had made what she thought was a deal. But when she had walked into the store that morning, he had changed his mind about how many jars of her new SunLite Coconut Hair Oil he wanted and the price he was willing to pay for each jar.

Trina tried to stay calm, but what he wanted was unfair and impossible. Trina and Queenie would lose money with what he was asking. Trina believed she knew what had happened. On the phone they had worked things out business person to business person. But once she arrived at the store and he saw that she was black and young, he decided she must be desperate. But he didn't know Trina Sims, and he certainly didn't know the woman who had raised her.

Trina had thanked him kindly for his time, gathered up her

box of jars, and put them back in the trunk of her car. The store manager looked as though he couldn't believe she would just walk out like that. He cursed her as she left. He would call every store in town and tell them not to stock her product, he yelled. He told her she would be ruined in a week. "All I needed this pretty morning was one more white man in a monkey suit taking me for a fool," Trina thought as she drove away.

She turned into the Moore Farm driveway, the dirt of the dusty road flying behind her. Jenny was sitting on her bags outside the guest house. Trina pulled around in a circle and stopped the car. She jumped out and opened the trunk.

"Are you trying to make me miss my train?" Jenny asked. She tucked her bag into the trunk.

Trina smiled at her. "Now, why would I do a thing like that? I was the one taking you where you needed to go all weekend."

The two women climbed into the car, and Trina drove off in another cloud of dust. "What time is it?" she asked, trying to steer and light a cigarette. Loose coals dropped into her lap. She slapped the sparks out and tried again to light the cigarette.

"12:25."

"What time is your train?"
"1:45," Jenny answered. She looked over at Trina. "Something must have come up, huh? You haven't been late once all weekend." Jenny was smiling, and she noticed that Trina was not. "Everything all right?"

"No. But it's okay. Because everything is a lesson, Jenny

Bryan. And I'm learning, learning, learning, new things every day. Don't worry. We'll get there in time." She took a long drag from the cigarette and noticed Jenny looking at her with something like disgust. "I don't want to talk about my morning," Trina said. "I want to talk about what you're going to do in two weeks. Nelson told me Mrs. Moore offered you the job."

"No secrets around this place, huh?" Jenny said.

"Oh, there are some, but that wasn't a secret. The people at the farm liked you a lot. They want you to take the job." She tapped Jenny on the leg as she teased, "They said if they couldn't have me there, they might as well have you." The two women laughed as the Buick eased off the dirt road and took up the blacktop that would lead them right to the train yard.

"Well?" Trina asked. "What do you think?"

"First, Trina Sims, I think you need to quit smoking."

Trina let out a mouthful of smoke and looked wide-eyed at Jenny.

"Where did that come from?" she asked.

Jenny's words stumbled and fell fast from her mouth. "I hate cigarettes. They stink up everything, and more than that, they kill you. Back at my hospital job I worked with a lot of coal miners and long-time smokers, and let me tell you, lung cancer ain't pretty work, Trina. And—I care about you," she said.

Trina wasn't looking at Jenny anymore. "I haven't been smoking that long," she said. "Just started last year—I'm not sure why."

"Well, before the hair oil business takes off real good and you start flying around the country in your Wonder Woman jet and you find you really need a cigarette to ease the stress, just let it go." She turned and looked right into those sunglasses. "All right?"

"Maybe." Trina took the cigarette she was smoking and crushed it into the ashtray. "I guess I just haven't been thinking."

"Hey! Just like me back in Stone Creek. Before you took me to Luketown."

Trina looked at her and smiled.

"You just don't know," Jenny said. "What I saw on my own really made me think. Instead of just believing what I've always been told without questioning it. And talking to you. It was like somebody opened my eyes up and poured in something real for a change."

"I could see it when you got off the train," Trina said. "You weren't hateful. You just came from a hateful place. Sorta like that cigarette I just put out—I just never really thought about how stupid it was."

"So why'd you take me there?" Jenny asked. "I mean, I wouldn't even shake your hand—"

"Because something told me you needed this job. With all those black and brown people out at Mrs. Moore's farm, the only way you were going to get the job was if you learned something real about black people and something real about yourself. I knew I couldn't tell you. You had to see it for yourself. That's just human nature, I guess."

They rode quietly for a while, looking at things along the road, each lost in her own thoughts. The only radio station they could get was country and western. "If you have to go on and leave me, please don't forget to send me your change of address," sang some lonesome cowboy. Trina sang along in a high voice that mocked the singer's throaty sound. Trina laughed out loud. She realized Jenny wasn't laughing with her. She was hugging herself and playing with the sleeves of that same yellow sweater.

"I'm hurrying," she said. "We're almost there. What's wrong with you all of the sudden? You don't like silly love songs?"

"Love is silly, that's all," she said.

"Hey, you're right about that. So, are you taking the job or not?"

"Yeah, I'm taking it."

"All right, Miss Jenny! Yes!" Trina hit the steering wheel and blew the car horn twice. The cows in the fields looked up at the baby blue Wildcat as it noisily sped past.

Jenny thought about the way Trina said you leave Luketown and hugged herself a little tighter.

"That's good. Really good," Trina said. She noticed Jenny wasn't smiling about the news. As they got closer to the train station, Jenny held herself tighter and tighter, pulling on her sweater sleeves and frowning. Trina noticed the green and yellow of fading bruises on her arms. Her fingers went over to Jenny's arm and lifted up the cuff of the sweater. She took off her sunglasses and put them on the seat between them.

"You gonna be okay when you get back?" Her eyes were full of questions as they darted from Jenny's arms and up to her eyes and back.

"I don't know. I didn't come all this way just to find a job, Trina. I came this far because I need to get away from Billy Joe. That's my husband. And women in Stone Creek just don't leave their husbands—they marry for life. But it's getting real bad. And I don't want to end up dead. So, no—between now and two weeks from now, I don't know if I'm going to be all right. But I know I'm leaving him. That much I do know. And I gotta plan too. Mama always said, 'No matter what you do, always have a plan.'"

"You got a good plan or a bad plan?"

Jenny dropped her head and smiled. "I think I got a good plan. I been working on it for a long time. This was the last piece I needed to put in place. I decided I wasn't going to take any more hits. That was the hard part. Then I just needed somewhere to go."

"I don't suppose I could be too much help to you. Me, with my dark, pretty self wouldn't go over too good in Stone Creek." Trina picked up the sunglasses from the seat and slid them back on.

"You know what, Trina? I can't explain it exactly—but when I stepped off that train three days ago, I felt so helpless. I didn't know what in the world I was doing. I could feel myself moving, but I didn't know for sure where I was going. I was scared. But something happened in all this moving around with you. I don't feel helpless anymore. Maybe because I finally did something—something that I've never done before—and the sun didn't fall out of the sky. Everything was still standing after I did it."

"That'll do it, Girl. That'll do it every time. Why, just this morning a thief of a man offered me 50 cents a jar for something my mama made with her own two hands and 20 years of her life. I told him, 'No thank you,' and I walked out of his office. My back felt so wide that I thought I had grown two or three backbones just that quick. But when I got out to the car and put my hand back there and felt around, I smiled to myself because I still only had one. But it was all mine, with nothing borrowed from anybody else."

When they pulled up, the southbound train was already there and had started loading its passengers. They had less than ten minutes before it pulled off. After Jenny got her bag from the trunk, Trina handed her a small package wrapped in brown paper.

"I ran out of pretty paper and had to use a grocery sack, but remember what they say. It's not what's outside that counts, it's what's inside."

Jenny put down her suitcase and took the package. She couldn't find the words she wanted to thank Trina for all she had done. She pulled the tape back and a pair of sunglasses slipped out into her hand followed by a piece of colorful paper. It was a handmade coupon with big handwriting that read, "Mr. Ben's Gift Certificate. Good for one FREE Catfish Dinner. Luketown store only."

"Don't you never, ever, feel helpless again, Jenny Bryan. You hear me? Never ever. You can feel confused or happy or hungry or full or scared, but not helpless. You are not helpless in this world. There are good folks everywhere. You just have to find them."

Jenny reached up and put her arms around Trina's shoulders. "And when you wear those sunglasses," Trina said, "you can even keep or tell a secret every now and then. If you want to. I repeat, if you want to."

Jenny was shaking. Trina gave her one of those royal hugs that the Queen had taught her to give so that people always want another one when they see you again. "Two weeks, Jenny Bryan," she said. "I'll be right back here in two weeks to give you a ride."

"And maybe I'll get to meet your mama and thank her in person for that coconut pie." The train whistle blew that one last longest time.

Jenny gave the man in the blue cap her bag and stepped onto the train. She turned away for a minute, then turned back and waved at Trina, who was resting on the warm hood of the baby blue Wildcat. Two pairs of dark glasses sparkled in the bright Kentucky sun, right at each other.

About the Author

Nikky Finney has been writing for as long as she has memory. She was born in Conway, South Carolina, in 1957. She was raised in several towns all across the state. Choosing to remain in her beloved South, she attended Talladega College in Alabama.

Her first book of poems, *On Wings of Gauze* (William Morrow), was published in 1985. A second book, *Rice* (Sister Vision, Black Women and Women of Color Press), came out in 1995. She has also published in numerous journals and anthologies.

Finney currently works and writes in Lexington, Kentucky, where she is a founding member of the Affrilachian Poets and associate professor of creative writing at the University of Kentucky.